Rodeo Rider

First published in 2009
by Wayland

Text copyright © Mick Gowar
Illustration copyright © François Hall

Wayland
338 Euston Road
London NW1 3BH

Wayland Australia
Level 17/207 Kent Street
Sydney, NSW 2000

Series Editor: Louise John
Cover design: Paul Cherrill
Design: D.R.ink
Consultants: Shirley Bickler

A CIP catalogue record for this book is available from the British Library.

ISBN 9780750255509

Printed in China

Wayland is a division of Hachette Children's Books,
an Hachette Livre UK Company

www.hachettelivre.co.uk

Rodeo Rider

Written by Mick Gowar
Illustrated by François Hall

WAYLAND

Everyone in Cactus Thorn was very excited. Buffalo Bob's Wild West Show had come to town.

"My Wild West Show is the greatest show on Earth!" said Buffalo Bob.

Sheriff Stan and Deputy Pete went to the show the first day it arrived. "Come on, Pete," said Stan. "Let's have a look around."

There were bareback riders. There was Clarice the Cow, made from real butter. And there was Mad Mickey the Mean Mustang.

"I'll give 100 dollars to anyone who can ride Mad Mickey!" shouted Buffalo Bob.

"Go on, Dudley," said Ma Dalton. "Have a go. We need the money."

Dudley climbed onto Mad Mickey. Mad Mickey's ears went back, his eyes rolled then he jumped...

...and he kicked.

Dudley Dalton flew through the air and landed right on top of Clarice the Cow. He slid to the floor, covered in sticky butter.

"Hoo-Hoo! Hee-Hee! Ha-Ha!" laughed
Sheriff Stan and Deputy Pete.

"Why don't YOU try riding Mad Mickey, then?" asked Ma Dalton.

"Oh, no! I'm not that stupid," said Sheriff Stan. "Come on, Pete, let's get an ice cream." Stan put Buckshot's hat on to keep the hot sun off his head, and they went to the ice cream stall.

"Sheriff Stan laughed at me," said
Dudley. "So did Deputy Pete."

"I've got a plan to get our own back," said Ma. "Look at Mad Mickey and Buckshot – they could be twins! Let's swap them around."

"But Mad Mickey has a white mark on his head," said Dudley.

"I know but we can put Buckshot's hat on Mickey's head, " said Ma. "They'll look exactly the same."

"Time to go home," said Sheriff Stan after the show. "Come on, Buckshot!"

Sheriff Stan jumped in the saddle.
Suddenly, Mad Mickey's ears went
back and his eyes rolled.

"What's the matter, Buckshot?"
asked Sheriff Stan.
Mad Mickey jumped...

...and he kicked.

But still Sheriff Stan held on.

"Stop right now, Buckshot!" shouted Sheriff Stan.

Mad Mickey twisted and kicked...

...and off flew his cowboy hat.

But still Sheriff Stan held on.

"That's not Buckshot!" shouted Deputy Pete. "It's Mad Mickey! Sheriff Stan's riding Mad Mickey!"

"Sheriff Stan, you've won 100 dollars!" shouted Buffalo Bob. "You're the greatest rodeo rider in the Wild West!"

"Yahoo!" cried Stan.

"Time to go home," said Deputy Pete. "Here's the real Buckshot."

"Ooh, I think I'll walk," said Sheriff Stan. "No more horse-riding for me today!"

31

START READING is a series of highly enjoyable books for beginner readers. **The books have been carefully graded to match the Book Bands widely used in schools.** This enables readers to be sure they choose books that match their own reading ability.

Look out for the Band colour on the book in our Start Reading logo.

The Bands are:

Pink Band 1

Red Band 2

Yellow Band 3

Blue Band 4

Green Band 5

Orange Band 6

Turquoise Band 7

Purple Band 8

Gold Band 9

START READING books can be read independently or shared with an adult. They promote the enjoyment of reading through satisfying stories supported by fun illustrations.

Mick Gowar has written more than 70 books for children, and likes to visit schools and libraries to give readings and lead workshops. He has also written plays and songs, and has worked with many orchestras. Mick writes his books in a shed in Cambridge.

François Hall loves the Wild West, but lives in a terraced 'ranch' down in the South. As well as being quick on the draw, he also designs knitting books. Cowboys often knitted on the homestead and poor Dudley has to wear very itchy underpants made by Ma Dalton!